HANDS OFF BLAK KIDS

TELL THE TRUTH

TREATY! NOW

CHANGE THE DA
WE STI
WONT CELEBRAT

GINES
IM
ZEN
TS!

ABORIGINES
CONFERENCE
DAY of MOURNING

PAY THE RENT

this has black fu

is Land has a ck future

ALWAYS WAS ALWAYS WILL

ABOR
FE
Y of

ABORIGINES
CLAIM
CITIZEN
RIGHTS!

BORIGINES
NFERENCE

CHANGE THE DATE
WE STILL
WONT CELEBRA

TREATY NOW

PAY THE RENT
TREATY! NOW

ALWAYS WAS ALWAYS WILL BE

AUNTY FAY MUIR & SUE LAWSON

Bung
Yarnda.

This is a Magabala Book

LEADING PUBLISHER OF ABORIGINAL AND
TORRES STRAIT ISLANDER STORYTELLERS.

CHANGING THE WORLD, ONE STORY AT A TIME.

First published 2024, reprinted 2025
Magabala Books Aboriginal Corporation
1 Bagot Street, Broome, Western Australia
Website: www.magabala.com
Email: sales@magabala.com

Magabala Books is assisted by the Australian Government through Creative Australia, its principal arts investment and advisory body. The State of Western Australia has made an investment in this project through the Department of Local Government, Sport and Cultural Industries. Magabala Books would also like to acknowledge Reconciliation Australia.

Magabala Books is Australia's only independent Aboriginal and Torres Strait Islander publishing house. Magabala Books acknowledges the Traditional Owners of the Country on which we live and work. We recognise the unbroken connection to traditional lands, waters and cultures. Through what we publish, we honour all our Elders, peoples and stories, past, present and future.

Design and typesetting by Emilia Toia
Printed in China by Everbest Printing Company

ISBN 978-1-922777-61-4 (Print)
ISBN 978-1-922777-60-7 (ePDF)

A catalogue record for this book is available from the National Library of Australia

Previous pages: NAIDOC march 1992, on the steps of Parliament House, Naarm/Melbourne.

FOREWORD

This book contains stories of resistance that the authors believe need to be told respectfully and from First Nations people's perspectives.

The authors have taken great care to focus on sourcing information written by First Nations people and families connected to noted figures and events, as well as their reflections and recollections.

History writing is a complex and ongoing process. The authors view *Always Was, Always Will Be* as a work in progress. All efforts have been made to ensure accuracy, but we will always make space for other voices. If you are concerned about any of the information presented, have queries or have more details to share, please contact Magabala Books.

Thanks to Maxine Briggs, Cole Baxter, the Wangka Maya Pilbara Aboriginal Language Centre, Reconciliation Australia, the Australian Institute of Aboriginal and Torres Strait Islander Studies, Wurundjeri Woi Wurrung Cultural Heritage Aboriginal Corporation, Anny Druett, David Jago, Dean Freeman, Maree Clarke, Fran Edmonds, Alannah Croom, Meredith Burgmann, Rachel Perkins and Natalie Ironfield for assistance with the text and images for this work.

CHANGE THE DATE
WE STILL
WONT CELEBRATE
ALWAYS WAS
ALWAYS WILL BE
PAY THE RENT
this land has a black future
TREATY! NOW
TREATY
SOVEREIGNTY
230 YEARS RENT
ALWAYS WAS
ALWAYS WILL BE

Opposite: Invasion Day march in Naarm/Melbourne, 2019.

NIKE
AIR

INTRODUCTION

Australia is a democratic country. In a democracy, people elect politicians to form government and run the country. Australia's democratic system is based on core values. These include the freedom to vote, stand for election, gather in groups, freedom of religious belief and freedom of speech.

Freedom of speech is particularly powerful. It gives Australian citizens the right to protest if they feel a law, event or behaviour is unjust or unfair. By protesting, citizens put pressure on authorities, including politicians, to make changes. There are many ways to protest, including rallies, marches, petitions or letters to the media. The arts, including music, art, poetry and stories are also a powerful form of protest.

When it comes to civil rights and equality for Australia's First Nations people, protests have achieved great change. Many people today see current campaigns as new ideas, but a look at history shows us First Nations people have been fighting for equal rights since Europeans first arrived in Botany Bay.

Opposite: NAIDOC march 1992, Fitzroy, Wurundjeri Country.

EUROPEAN ARRIVAL

In 1788, when the First Fleet arrived, more than 300,000 Aboriginal people lived in clans across Australia. Each clan belonged to one of approximately 250 nations. Clans had their own language and shared similar laws, customs and culture.

Aboriginal people, though wary, initially welcomed the newcomers. Many clans and individuals helped Europeans find food, water and shelter and often saved lives. However, their feelings of welcome and generosity changed once it became clear Europeans didn't understand or respect Aboriginal people and culture. As more and more Europeans arrived and took over their land, First Nations people knew they had to do something to protect their food and water sources, sacred sites and clans. They began to resist takeover of their Country. The methods to protest European presence and behaviour varied, from refusal to adopt the newcomers' way, to violent resistance.

For example, Barangaroo, wife of Wangal man Bennelong, refused to wear European clothes or eat their food. She even stopped a whipping she felt was cruel. Bidjigal man Pemulwuy attacked stock and buildings to protest the takeover of his land. Later he attacked Europeans who mistreated his people. And Whadjuk man Yagan fought back when white settlers went unpunished for killing an Aboriginal boy. These are just a few examples amongst hundreds of incidents where clan members all over the country protested to change what was happening.

Despite the brave and persistent efforts, Europeans kept coming. With their growing numbers and superior weapons, they defeated any First Nations resistance.

For many decades, representations of European arrival did not include the experiences of First Nations people.

As time passed, First Nations people learnt more about European people and their way of life. They discovered that Europeans had different attitudes to the environment. Unlike Aboriginal people who had a strong oral tradition, Europeans valued the written word.

First Nations people knew if they were to protect their people and Country, they had to learn to read and write English. This would allow them to use the written word to protest and ask for change. By the mid-1800s, leaders like William Cooper and William Barak had written letters and gathered signatures for petitions asking for changes to the treatment of First Nations people.

CORANDERRK STATION, VICTORIA

The European takeover of First Nation people's Country in Victoria was swift and violent. White settlers, who began arriving in 1835, were eager to claim land to build wealth. They had little understanding of First Nations people and little interest in their way of life or connection to land. Settlers made it clear Aboriginal people weren't welcome and built fences that blocked access to land, food and water. The newcomers also attacked and killed entire clans if they broke the settlers' new rules. These attacks, as well as disease and starvation, devastated the First Nations population.

Billibellary was a Wurundjeri Elder, or in language, a Ngurungaeta. By 1840, he knew if his people were to survive, they had to find a new way to live. He petitioned Assistant Aboriginal Protector William Thomas, asking for land for the Wurundjeri people – a clan north of Melbourne – of the Kulin Nation, Victoria, to live on and farm. Thomas refused the request. Billibellary and the Elder who followed him, Simon Wonga, continued to petition for their own land.

On 30 June 1863, 20 years after Billibellary's initial request, the Victorian Government finally agreed to create an Aboriginal station near Healesville. The government allocated 2000 acres (803 hectares). This increased to 4830 acres (1954 hectares) when the station was successful. Wurundjeri Elders named the station Coranderrk after a plant growing in the area.

Kulin Nation Elders and the Victorian Board for the Protection of Aborigines (The Board) appointed Presbyterian Pastor and Board Inspector John Green as Coranderrk's first manager. The Board, which in 1863 was known as the Central Board Appointed to Watch Over the Interests of Aborigines, controlled Aboriginal people's lives.

Opposite: Residents of Coranderrk Station, Healesville, 1890.

ALWAYS WAS ALWAYS WILL BE

“All we want to do is live and die at Coranderrk.”

WILLIAM BARAK

Aboriginal people were pleased with The Board and their Elders' choice. They knew Green respected Aboriginal people and culture.

Green worked with Elders to set rules, regulations and punishments for Coranderrk residents. He helped unite clans from Victoria and southern New South Wales. Green encouraged the residents to adopt Christian ways, but unlike other station managers, he allowed them to continue some cultural practices. Under Green and the Elders' leadership, Coranderrk's population grew to more than 100 people by 1875.

Coranderrk became a thriving community and one of the most successful farms in the region. Residents cleared and fenced 700 acres (283 hectares), ran cattle, produced milk and grew hops. They also established a market garden and orchard and built homes, a dairy, bakery and other buildings. Coranderrk was a happy, safe and productive station.

However, the station's success did not please everyone. Local farmers began pressuring the government to give them the land so it could be farmed 'properly'. The Board kept Coranderrk's profits, which stopped residents from completing needed repairs and improvements. Board members also insisted Green employ white workers who, unlike the residents, would receive a wage.

When Green complained to The Board in 1874, it tricked him into resigning and appointed a new, cruel manager, Christian Ogilvie. Unlike Green, Ogilvie didn't respect First Nations people or their culture. Under Ogilvie, the quality and quantity of rations declined. He also banned residents from travelling to work so they could earn money to buy their own food. Coranderrk residents lost their freedom and their voice.

William Barak, who became Elder after Simon Wonga died, protested to The Board. He asked for Green's return and for residents to have more control over their lives and over Coranderrk. Barak wrote letters and sent petitions. When these were ignored, he and six other Coranderrk men walked 60 kilometres to Melbourne to speak to Board members. The Board refused his requests and conditions at Coranderrk became worse.

Opposite: Wurundjeri leader and political activist William Barak, age 33.

Desperate to improve his people's lives, Barak again walked to Melbourne and back. However, instead of The Board, Barak met with Chief Secretary Graham Berry. After this meeting, The Board replaced Ogilvie with Hugh Halliday.

But, Halliday was no different than Ogilvie, so Barak and a group of men returned to Melbourne to meet with Berry once again. After the meeting, The Board replaced Halliday with Reverend Strickland. Strickland, who was quick to anger, cruel and violent, had little understanding of farming and less of Aboriginal culture. Life at Coranderrk became unbearable. Desperate for change, the residents went on strike.

Despite suffering with a broken leg, Barak again returned to Melbourne on foot. He and the 22 residents who accompanied him, stayed at the Kew home of Barak's friend, Board member Ann Bon. When Barak again met with Berry, Barak detailed Strickland's cruel treatment and asked for Green to be returned as manager. Barak also stressed his people's wish to stay at Coranderrk and continue to work on and care for the land. After this meeting, Berry set up the 1881 Parliamentary Coranderrk Inquiry. This was the only inquiry in the 1800s into the treatment and living conditions of Victorian Aboriginal people.

The inquiry, which ran for two and a half months, heard from more than 60 witnesses, including 24 Coranderrk residents, John Green and Strickland. Barak's petition stated:

"We want only one man here, and that is Mr John Green, and the station to be under the Chief Secretary; then we will show the country that the station could self-support itself."

The inquiry's report agreed Strickland had to be replaced. It also recommended more attention be paid to the station and that hop production, which was particularly successful, increase. The Aborigines Protection Board, as it was now known, replaced Strickland with William Goodall but ignored the inquiry's other recommendations.

Coranderrk Station was a thriving and productive Aboriginal farming enterprise.

In 1883, Barak returned to Melbourne to speak to Berry. Barak was delighted when the Chief Secretary recommended Coranderrk become a permanent place for Aboriginal people. Before Berry retired, Barak returned to Melbourne a last time to thank and farewell the Chief Secretary.

Instead of following Berry's recommendations the Victorian Government introduced the 1886 Half-Caste Act. This Act meant that any person under the age of 35 and not considered to be a 'full' Aboriginal could not continue to live in Victoria's six missions. The Act also allowed for the removal of children from their families.

With the young and fit expelled from Coranderrk, the station fell into further disrepair. It turned from a thriving, successful community into a quiet village with a population of fewer than 40.

Barak stayed at Coranderrk and continued to fight for his people's rights until he died in 1903, aged 80. Throughout his life, Barak remained friends with John Green and his family. Today, Barak is remembered as a determined, wise leader who acted as a bridge between two worlds.

ALWA
WAS
ALWA
WILL B

THE OPENING OF PROVISIONAL PARLIAMENT HOUSE, CANBERRA

9 MAY 1927

The first recorded Aboriginal protest at Parliament House, Canberra, occurred on 9 May 1927.

From Federation, 1 January 1901, until May 1927, Australia's Federal Parliament sat in Melbourne at Victoria's Parliament House. During this time, the Federal Government chose Canberra as the site for Federal Parliament House and built a 'Provisional Parliament House'. The government's intended larger and grander permanent Parliament House wasn't built for another 61 years. In 1988, the current Parliament House in Canberra replaced Provisional Parliament House, now known as Old Parliament House.

The future king, Prince Albert, Duke of York, opened Provisional Parliament House on 9 May 1927. The opening was a grand, formal event. Troops marched, the army band played and renowned Australian singer Dame Nellie Melba sang God Save The

Opposite: Activist Jimmy Clements standing in front of police at Parliament House, 1927.

King. Invited dignitaries and members of the public filled grandstands. Despite the planning, an important group of people was not invited – the traditional custodians of the land – the Wiradjuri, a large clan from central New South Wales.

The lack of invitation didn't stop Wiradjuri Elders Jimmy 'King Billy' Clements and John 'Marvellous' Noble from attending. Clements, also known as Nangar, and Noble walked more than 150 kilometres from Brungle Aboriginal Mission, situated on Wiradjuri Country, near Tumut, over mountains to Canberra. When they arrived, barefoot, in dusty suits and with their dogs, Clements and Noble stood on the Parliament House steps and asked to be presented to the Duke and Duchess of York. The elderly men wanted to show Aboriginal people's ownership of the land and highlight their poor living conditions.

Police tried again and again to remove the men, declaring that Clements and Noble were uninvited and inappropriately dressed. The Wiradjuri men stood their ground. Reports say Clements declared he was standing on his own land.

The large crowd turned on police, urging them to allow the men to stay. Eventually, the police backed down. Thanks to the crowd's support, Clements and Noble not only stayed for the ceremony, but met the Duke and Duchess of York. After the ceremony, Clements, Noble and their dogs walked back to Tumut. Three months later, 80-year-old Jimmy Clements died at Queanbeyan.

Today, Clements and Noble's action is remembered as the first Aboriginal Australian protest at Australia's Federal Parliament House.

Opposite: Jimmy Clements in front of Parliament House, 1927.

ABORIGINES
CLAIM
CITIZEN
RIGHTS!
ABORIGINES
CONFERENCE
DAY of MOURNING
ABORIGINES
ABORIGINES
CLAIM
CITIZEN
RIGHTS!

DAY OF MOURNING, NEW SOUTH WALES

26 JANUARY 1938

Australia Day is held on 26 January, the anniversary of the First Fleet's arrival in New South Wales in 1788. Australia Day is intended as a celebration of our nation's people and the country's success and growth. However, for Australia's First Nations people, 26 January doesn't represent progress and growth. Rather, it represents the start of great sorrow and loss.

When Europeans arrived in Australia, many First Nations people lost their Country, language and culture. Thousands of people died. In recent times, the push to change the date and how we acknowledge Australia Day has become stronger. This protest against the day isn't a new idea. First Nations people's first formal protested celebration of 26 January occurred in 1938.

On 26 January 1938, when Sydney celebrated 150 years since the First Fleet's arrival, a group of Aboriginal people gathered for a Day of Mourning. The Day of Mourning was organised by Yorta Yorta – a clan from country Victoria – Elder William Cooper, Yorta Yorta activist Jack Patten and Wiradjuri Elder Bill Ferguson. These men spent their lives fighting to raise awareness of the unfair treatment of First Nations people.

Opposite: Activists of the Aboriginal Advancement League. Left to right: William Ferguson, Jack Kinchela, Isaac Ingram, Doris Williams, Esther Ingram, Arthur Williams, Phillip Ingram, Louis Agnes Ingram OAM holding daughter Olive Ingram, Jack Patten, unknown woman, around the time of the Day of Mourning protest in 1938.

In 1932, aged 72, William Cooper together with Marge Tucker, Bill Onus and Doug Nichols began the Victorian-based Australian Aborigines' League (AAL).

Ferguson, who had been an organiser for the Australian Workers' Union, also fought against unfair treatment of First Nations people, particularly when it came to wages. In 1937, Ferguson helped form the New South Wales-based Aborigines Progressive Association (APA) from his home town in Dubbo.

In 1938, the government announced a parade and re-enactment to celebrate the 150th anniversary of the First Fleet's arrival. Cooper, Ferguson and Patten joined forces with other First Nation's leaders to organise the Australian Aborigines Conference: Sesquicentenary Day of Mourning and Protest. This was the first Aboriginal protest organised by Australia's traditional owners from different states.

As the 150th celebrations began on 26 January, more than 100 Aboriginal people stood in silent protest outside Sydney Town Hall. Once the sesquicentenary parade passed, the protesters marched to Australia Hall for the conference. Only four non-Aboriginal people – two policemen and two newspaper photographers – attended.

At the conference, Chairman Jack Patten called for better education, full citizenship and voting rights for Aboriginal and Torres Strait Islander people. He also called for the end of Aboriginal Protection Boards. After the event, protestors travelled to La Perouse where they floated wreaths out to sea. The wreaths, prepared by Ngemba woman Pearl Gibbs, were a memorial to the First Nations people who'd died since 1788.

Opposite: William Cooper, one of the leaders of the Day of Mourning, which protested celebrations being held on 26 January 1938.

ALWAYS
WAS
ALWAYS
WILL BE

Five days after the conference, a delegation of 20 Aboriginal leaders, including Ferguson and Cooper, met with Prime Minister Joseph Lyons, his wife Enid and Minister for the Interior, John McEwen. The delegation presented the politicians with a list of 10 demands, including a request for full citizenship rights for First Nations people.

Following the meeting, Protection Boards changed, but little else did. It took decades for First Nations people to receive the vote and full citizenship rights. Cooper, Ferguson and Patten weren't alive when these changes took place.

In 1940, two years after the Day of Mourning, William Cooper declared the Sunday before 26 January a day of celebration and protest. He named it National Aborigines Day. Fifteen years later, in 1955, National Aborigines Day's date changed to the first Sunday in July. Over time, the day evolved into what we now celebrate as NAIDOC Week. NAIDOC stands for National Aboriginal and Islanders' Day Observance Committee. The week is celebrated in the first week of July.

Nearly 80 years after the Day of Mourning, Australia's First Nations people continue to argue for 26 January to be called Invasion Day or Survival Day.

“We have been ‘protected’ for 150 years and look what has become of us.”

WILLIAM BARAK

NIGHT OF BROKEN GLASS PROTEST, VICTORIA

6 DECEMBER 1938

Kristallnacht, the Night of Broken Glass, marked the start of Nazi Germany's persecution of Jewish people during World War II. In 1938, after a Jewish youth killed a German official in Paris, Third Reich soldiers and civilians attacked Jewish businesses, homes, synagogues and people across Germany and Austria. The attack lasted two days, over 9–10 November. The brutal and violent attacks destroyed more than 800 businesses and set homes and synagogues on fire. More than 30,000 Jewish men, women and children were arrested. The official death toll was 36, however the actual toll is thought to be much higher.

Even though the violent attack was reported worldwide, very few protests occurred. One of those protests in Australia was organised by Yorta Yorta man William Cooper and his fellow members of the Australian Aborigines' League (AAL).

After learning about the Night of Broken Glass, 77-year-old Cooper, known for his dedication to improving Aboriginal Australian's lives, collected signatures for a petition against the violence. On 6 December 1938, without transportation or money for train fares, Cooper and a group of the Australian Aborigines' League members

Opposite: An excerpt from the petition written by William Cooper to the German Consul in 1938, reproduced on the inscription of a statue of William on Yorta Yorta Country, Queens Gardens Shepparton.

walked from Cooper's home in Footscray to the German Consulate offices on Collins Street, Melbourne. Here, they tried to meet with German Consul-General R.W. Dreschler and present him with their petition. Dreschler refused to see them.

Even though the protestors felt their efforts hadn't made a difference, their protest is considered to be one of the first against the Nazi regime.

Despite Dreschler's refusal to meet them, the protesters managed to highlight the treatment of Jewish people in Germany and at the same time, shine a light on Australia's treatment of First Nations people. In 2010, the Yad Vashem Holocaust Museum in Jerusalem dedicated a memorial in the museum's garden in memory of William Cooper and his stand against the treatment of Jewish people.

"On behalf of the Aboriginal inhabitants of Australia we wish to have it registered and on record that we protest wholeheartedly at the cruel persecution of the Jewish people by the Nazi government in Germany. We plead that you would make it known to your government and its military leaders that this cruel persecution of their fellow citizens must be brought to an end."

From the letter that was planned to be presented to the German Consul.

CUMMERAGUNJA WALK OFF, NEW SOUTH WALES AND VICTORIA

4 FEBRUARY 1939

In the late 1800s, Maloga Mission, near Moama, New South Wales, was a harsh place to live. The religious manager believed in strict rules, hard work and firm punishment. Residents weren't paid for their work. In 1874, Maloga residents wrote the first of two petitions to the NSW Government. The petitions asked for less government control over their lives and for ownership of their own land. The Yorta Yorta people didn't want to live on handouts. They wanted to be self-sufficient. The government ignored their request.

By 1881, conditions at Maloga had become even worse. 42 men, including William Cooper who spent his teenage years at Maloga, wrote a second petition. This petition again asked for 100 acres (40 hectares) of land to live on and farm. This petition and the many letters Cooper wrote to politicians and newspapers at the time are seen as the beginning of his activism.

Two years after receiving the second petition, the NSW Government agreed to set aside 1800 acres (728 hectares) of land for an Aboriginal station on the Murray River, near the Victorian town of Barmah. The station was named Cummeragunja Station. Cummeragunja is a Yorta Yorta word meaning 'our home'.

Opposite: Cooper and his colleagues, friends and allies used leafletting as part of their actions.

THE FIGHT AT CUMMERAGUNJA

Aborigines In Protest

Leave Government Supervised Camp
And Set Up STRIKE CAMP At
BARMAH - VICTORIA
(ON THE BANKS OF THE MURRAY)

Although supposedly reserved for the benefit of the aborigines, Cummerangunja's 3000 acres of fertile land, cleared by the aborigines, have been leased by the Government to squatters and pastoralists, with the exception of 60 acres, upon which are congested the 320 aborigines.

The 320 were forced to live in 35 two-roomed huts and four bag shelters.

Self-respect is undermined by "dole" living.

Starvation follows weekly rations, valued for adults at 3/5, for children 1/8½.

Social, medical and educational services are insufficient and are so mal-administered as to add to the general misery.

THE ABORIGINES' ASSISTANCE COMMITTEE

WORKING IN CONJUNCTION WITH THE NATIVES' ORGANISATION
THE AUSTRALIAN ABORIGINES' LEAGUE

Is Organising An Immediate Relief Of Distress
And The Creation Of Supporting Public Opinion

THE HELP OF YOUR MONEY WILL WIN THEIR FIGHT

Industrial Print, 24 Victoria St., Carlton, N.3. (40-hour week)

Aborigines' Assistance Committee, 5th Floor (phone). Kurrajong House, Collins St. (near Metro Theatre).

The land was broken into 20-acre (8-hectare) blocks and distributed amongst Cummeragunja families. Despite the blocks being smaller than requested, residents soon produced grain, wool, dairy and wood products. They cleared, fenced and farmed the land and built sheds and other buildings. By 1908, more than 300 people lived and worked on Cummeragunja Mission.

Though conditions were better than at Maloga, the residents still received no pay for their work. Instead, they received rations of flour, sugar, tea and meat offcuts. Elders approached the NSW Board for the Protection of Aborigines to ask for pay and for better rations. The Board ignored their requests.

Conditions became worse in 1909 when the government introduced the NSW Aborigines Protection Act. As had happened at other stations, including Coranderrk, people under 35 who didn't fit the government's 'full aborigine' status were expelled from the station. Cummeragunja was left without young, fit workers. Before long, the effects of malnutrition, illness, neglect and manager Adrian McQuiggan's harsh treatment forced Cummeragunja residents to take a stand.

Family members invited former resident Jack Patten, who'd chaired the Sydney 1938 Day of Mourning conference, to speak to Cummeragunja residents about why they needed to protest. Before he could address the crowd, police arrested Patten for breaking NSW Aborigine Protection Board rules.

On 4 February 1939, days after Patten's arrest, 200 of the 300 Cummeragunja residents walked off the station and the land they had worked so hard to farm, to settle at Barmah in Victoria. Yorta Yorta people were so desperate for change that they'd rather walk off the station they'd fought for than live in such harsh and cruel conditions. Those who walked off refused to return to Cummeragunja until McQuiggan was sacked, conditions improved and residents were allowed to travel without permission from white managers.

The Cummeragunja Walk Off was a significant mass protest. It lasted nine months, ending only when The Board removed McQuiggan from the station. Despite McQuiggan's removal, most of those who left Cummeragunja remained in camps on the Victorian side of the river at Barmah. Others settled in nearby towns Mooroopna and Shepparton.

Many First Nations activists, including William Cooper, Margaret Tucker, Geraldine Briggs and Jack Patten, supported the Cummeragunja Walk Off and continued to fight for fair and equal treatment of Aboriginal people.

On 9 March 1984, the title deeds for the Cummeragunja land passed to the Yorta Yorta people through the newly created Yorta Yorta Land Council. Descendants of the original residents still live at Cummeragunja today.

living condition was no good, we camp in the riverbed, no house. That's why we went on strike, not enough money, we working hard, hard life.

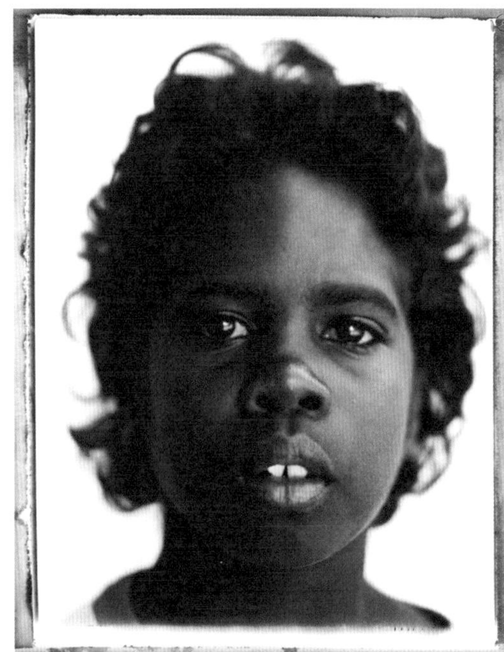

the strike made me proud

PILBARA STRIKE, WESTERN AUSTRALIA

On 1 May 1946, Aboriginal pastoral workers from Western Australia's Pilbara region walked off their jobs to strike for better pay and conditions. The strike is the longest in Australia's history.

Early in the twentieth century, cattle, sheep and cropping station owners employed more than 800 First Nations people as stockmen, farmhands and house servants. Station owners were also called pastoralists.

The 1936 Native Administration Act was meant to improve conditions for Aboriginal workers. The act made it a legal requirement for station owners to provide housing and medical services for workers and their families. However, the law wasn't enforced. Workers continued to be paid in rations of flour, sugar, tea and beef offcuts and housed in corrugated tin shacks without floors, electricity, furniture, cooking facilities or running water.

In 1944, fed up with poor conditions and treatment, Aboriginal men from 26 language groups held meetings across the Pilbara. They decided Aboriginal workers would strike until pastoralists met their demands. The workers wanted a wage of 30 shillings a week, to elect their own representatives and permission to leave stations without their employer's permission. Those at the meetings elected Nyangumarta Elder Dooley Bin Bin to represent the inland desert people and Nyamal Elder Clancy McKenna to represent the coastal people. They chose white man Don McLeod to liaise with the

Opposite: Teddy Allan and Dylan Corbett comment on the 1946 Pilbara Strike. Artwork exhibited in the *Lasting Legacy: 75th Anniversary of the Pilbara Strike* exhibition, 2021.

pastoralists and government officials. Aboriginal women, including Nyangumarta woman Daisy Bindi, also played an important role in the strike.

The organisers decided to begin the strike on 1 May – May Day – which is a worldwide celebration that commemorates the struggle for workers' rights. This date was also the day shearing season began in the Pilbara. This ensured the strike hit pastoralists hard.

The next challenge facing the group was how to spread news of the strike across the vast Pilbara. A large, dry area in the north of Western Australia, the Pilbara is twice as big as the state of Victoria. The solution involved a bicycle and jam-tin labels.

One of the leaders, Dooley Bin Bin, rode an old bicycle from one pastoral station to the next. At each station he told workers about the strike and left calendars on jam tin labels so workers knew when to stop work.

Though it is said the strike began on 1 May 1946, Aboriginal workers and their families began to walk off more than 20 Pilbara Stations from late April. The strikers set up two main camps. Nyamal Elder Clancy McKenna led the camp at 12 Mile Camp outside Port Hedland. Dooley Bin Bin led the other camp, called Moolyella, near Marble Bar.

At the camps, strikers not only hunted for food, they sold pearl shells and kangaroo and goat skins to raise money to pay for other supplies. They also used traditional methods to mine for precious minerals, which they sold.

The strikers, who believed that their children needed to be able to speak, write and read English, also established Australia's first bilingual Aboriginal schools. These children could already speak up to eight languages.

For the Pilbara's pastoralists who relied on First Nation people's knowledge and skill, the lack of workers meant reduced income. Desperate to end the strike, they sought support from the police.

Police arrested strike leaders McLeod, Bin Bin and McKenna, in the hope that the arrests would force strikers back to their jobs. Even though Bin Bin and McKenna spent three months in jail, the strike continued. McLeod was charged and tried seven times during the strike.

As the action continued, support amongst churches, unions and the Australian public grew. When the Seamen's Union stopped transporting wool from the Pilbara, the pastoralists' income dried up. In response, the Western Australian Government agreed to the strikers' demands, as long as the unions handled Pilbara wool again.

It took High Court intervention for the government to honour the promise to allow Aboriginal workers to elect their own leaders and representatives. Pastoralists didn't change. They refused requests for wages of 30 shillings per week and for the freedom to travel without permission.

Official records state the strike ended in 1949, however, not all workers returned to the stations. Some strikers did, but others found different jobs or continued to live a traditional life.

The Pilbara strike resulted in many big changes for Aboriginal people. It led the way for them to establish independent communities and schools in the Pilbara and for pastoral leases of their own. Many of the schools and communities established during the strike continue today. Across Australia, the Pilbara strike inspired First Nations people, showing them action and change was possible.

FEDERAL COUNCIL FOR THE ADVANCEMENT OF ABORIGINES AND TORRES STRAIT ISLANDERS (FCAATSI)

In 1956, a report into the living conditions and health of First Nations people in Western Australia's Warburton Ranges stunned Australians. The Grayden Report found those living in the Warburton Ranges suffered from malnutrition, blindness and disease and lived in appalling conditions.

The report's findings led to the formation of the Federal Council for Aboriginal Advancement (FCAA). Officially formed in Adelaide in 1958, FCAA aimed to be a unified voice for equal rights, the vote and for changes to the Constitution.

Members of FCAA, including Faith Bandler, Joe McGuinness and Doug Nicholls, had been working on the problem of voting rights for First Nations people since the early 1950s as part of the Aboriginal-Australian Fellowship. Now, they began to campaign harder for Aboriginal people to be allowed to vote in all elections. They also campaigned for changes to the Constitution to recognise Aboriginal people as Australian citizens. Group members held public meetings and met with politicians,

Opposite: A FCAATSI poster to support the 1967 Referendum to recognise Aboriginal and Torres Strait Island people in the Constitution.

community leaders and the media. They distributed petitions asking for equal rights for Australia's First Nations people.

In 1965, the organisation changed its name from FCAA to Federal Council for the Advancement of Aborigines and Torres Strait Islanders (FCAATSI). This change showed that the group represented not only Aboriginal people, but also Torres Strait Island people.

After winning the right to vote for First Nation people, FCAATSI members Faith Bandler, Charles Perkins, Pearl Gibbs and Oodgeroo Noonuccal (Kath Walker) turned their attention to changing Australia's Constitution to recognise First Nations people as Australian citizens. Their persistence and hard work led to the successful 1967 referendum in which Australians overwhelmingly voted to count Aboriginal people as part of the population and changes to the Constitution.

"Let us put in our time for human rights and let us live toward that. This is what I want people to remember."

PEARL GIBBS

Faith Bandler

Born in Tumbulgum NSW, civil rights activist Faith Bandler helped form the Aboriginal Australian Fellowship in 1956. The fellowship worked to improve First Nations people's rights. In 1958, Bandler joined FCAA and was general secretary from 1970–1973. She received the Order of Australia Medal in 1984 for service to Aboriginal welfare, the 1997 Human Rights Medal and was made a Companion of the Order of Australia in 2009. She died on 13 February 2015.

Pearl 'Gambanyi' Gibbs

Pearl Gibbs, born in 1901 at La Perouse, Sydney, fought to improve conditions for First Nations people, particularly women and children. Gibbs began working for First Nations people's rights in the 1930s and co-founded the Australian Aborigines' League. She helped organise the 1938 Day of Mourning. Gibbs was the first Aboriginal person and woman to became a member of the NSW Aborigines' Welfare Board. Along with Faith Bandler, Gibbs founded the Aboriginal Australian Fellowship, was a member of FCAATSI and a leading figure in establishing the Aboriginal Tent Embassy in 1972. She died on 28 April 1983.

THE RIGHT TO VOTE

After years of hard work and persistence, Australian women won the right to vote in federal elections in 1902. The battle for Australia's First Nations people's right to vote, though just as determined, took longer.

From the 1850s, when the British Government made most of Australia's colonies self-governing, all males over 21, including First Nations men, were eligible to vote. Many First Nation people didn't know or understand they were eligible to vote. When the Australian Constitution became law on 1 January 1901 to create the Commonwealth of Australia, First Nations men's right to vote changed.

Federation made each colony a state or territory, with its own government. The Australian Government governed all states and territories. When the Constitution became law, eligibility to vote became complicated. The new Australian Government introduced laws which prevented First Nations men from voting in federal elections unless they were already on the electoral roll.

While First Nations men in Tasmania, Victoria, South Australia and New South Wales could vote in state elections, they couldn't vote in Queensland and Western Australian elections.

Aboriginal rights organisations, such as the Australian Aborigines' League and Australian Aboriginal Progressive Association, demanded the same voting rights for First Nations people as for non-First Nations people. Despite their efforts, nothing changed until after World War II.

Soldiers returning from the war were upset to discover the Aboriginal and Torres Strait Islander men who had fought beside them couldn't vote. These soldiers pressured the Federal Government to change the law, arguing that if First Nations men were good enough to fight and die for their country, they were good enough to vote.

In 1949, the Australian Government changed voting laws to allow Aboriginal and Torres Strait Islander men who'd completed military service to vote. But, unlike non-First Nations people, voting wasn't compulsory.

Disappointed and frustrated, FCAA continued to lobby for equal voting rights for First Nations people. Finally, in 1962, the Menzies Government changed the Commonwealth Electoral Act to give Australia's traditional owners the right to vote. That same year, First Nations people in the Northern Territory and Western Australia also received the vote. The last state to introduce voting for Aboriginal people was Queensland in 1965.

It had been a long and tough battle, but FCAA knew there was more work to achieve equal rights for Australia's First Nations people.

Opposite: Harriet Ellis casts her referendum vote at the Sydney Town Hall voting booth, 1967.

ALWAYS
WAS
ALWAYS
WILL BE

> “We laid bare the strong prejudice against aborigines.”
>
> **CHARLES PERKINS**

THE AUSTRALIAN FREEDOM RIDES, NEW SOUTH WALES

12–26 FEBRUARY 1965

In 1964, a group of Australian university students protesting racial discrimination in the United States was surprised when they were criticised for not protesting about the treatment of Australia's First Nations people.

In response, Sydney university students formed Student Action for Aborigines (SAFA) to address and highlight racism against Australia's Aboriginal and Torres Strait Islander people. They elected Charles Perkins, an Arrernte and Kalkadoon man and first Aboriginal man to graduate from university, as president.

Inspired by the American civil rights protest in 1961, SAFA organised a bus trip through northern New South Wales towns, including Walgett, Moree, Bowraville, Kempsy and Lismore. The students wanted to talk to First Nations people and town residents to learn about treatment and conditions facing Aboriginal people and attitudes towards them. The students hoped to share what they discovered with all Australians.

With the help of Sydney pastor Reverend Ted Noffs, SAFA raised money to hire a bus. The group left Sydney on 12 February 1965. Over two weeks, the Freedom Ride

Opposite: Charles Perkins (fourth from left) stands with other activists next to the Student Action for Aborigines bus in Bowraville, NSW, 1965.

travelled 3200 kilometres and visited 21 towns. The 33 students on the bus, 11 women and 22 men, were all under 26 years of age. One student, Darce Cassidy, was a part-time reporter for the ABC. His reports and footage of the tour attracted national and international media attention.

The students were stunned by what they discovered. Aboriginal people lived on the outskirts of towns in houses without windows, doors, running water or toilets. They were refused service in town shops and cafes, barred from clubs, hotels and public pools and had to enter cinemas through back doors. Inside cinemas, they had to sit in special areas, usually on the floor. This segregation, known as the colour bar, was apartheid under another name.

After gathering information at several towns, the students held their first protest against the colour bar. They gathered outside the Walgett Returned Services League of Australia (RSL) where Aboriginal returned servicemen were refused membership. The students stood in the sun outside the RSL rooms, holding placards that read 'Walgett: Australia's Disgrace' and 'Bullets Didn't Discriminate'. After the protest, the students, originally welcomed to the town, were told to leave. That night, as the bus left town for Moree, a ute driven by a Walgett man forced the bus off the road and into a ditch. No-one was hurt and the shaken students continued their journey.

In Moree, the students protested outside the council-owned swimming pool. First Nations children were allowed to swim at the pool during school hours, but were banned after school. Darce Cassidy's reports on the Walgett RSL and Moree pool protests attracted much media attention.

While Perkins tried to enter the pool with Aboriginal children from the nearby settlement, the SAFA students stood outside the fence, holding placards. The pool manager refused Perkins and the children entry and called police. After a tense stand-off, the Moree Mayor, Bill Lloyd, met with Perkins and agreed to allow Aboriginal children to swim at the pool if the university students left town immediately. As soon

as the Freedom Riders left Moree, the colour bar was reinforced and the children were removed from the pool.

When SAFA learned what had occurred, the bus turned back to Moree. Again, the Freedom Riders protested, but this time locals threw rotten eggs, gravel, fruit and vegetables at them. Moree residents even attacked local man Bob Brown for supporting the students and First Nations people.

Again, the mayor and Perkins met. Perkins promised to leave when the colour bar was removed. This time the mayor stuck to his word. The Freedom Ride left Moree under police guard.

The Freedom Ride continued. Students protested in other towns, including Kempsey and Bowraville. At Bowraville, First Nations people had to enter the cinema via a back door labelled 'black only'. None of the other protests were as violent as Moree.

Student Action for Aborigines broke up in 1966 – one year after the Freedom Ride. The group achieved much in its short life, with mainstream media in Australia and overseas reporting on the issues of racism and discrimination. The Freedom Ride exposed rampant racism in Australia.

It is credited with encouraging Aboriginal people to stand against prejudice and influencing the 1967 referendum results, land rights battles and the Aboriginal Tent Embassy.

Perkins and Noffs formed the Foundation for Aboriginal Affairs in Sydney. In 1984, Perkins became the Secretary of the Department of Aboriginal Affairs, which advised the prime minister. Perkins continued to fight racism all his life and had an enormous impact on Australian society.

THE 1967 REFERENDUM

Before the 1967 referendum, the Australian Constitution mentioned Aboriginal and Torres Strait Islander people only twice. The first reference, in Section 51, stated that the Australian Government couldn't make laws or policies for Aboriginal people. The second, in Section 127, said Aboriginal Australians weren't to be counted in a population census.

When authorities wrote the Constitution they believed First Nations people were 'dying out' and therefore didn't need representation nor inclusion in the Constitution. This was clearly wrong and discriminated against Australia's traditional owners.

After achieving the vote for First Nations people, FCAA turned its attention to changing the Federal Constitution to recognise Aboriginal and Torres Strait Islander people. Group members, including Faith Bandler, Doug Nicholls, Charles Perkins and others, spoke to politicians, held rallies and collected signatures for petitions. They were interviewed for newspapers and appeared on television, all to raise awareness of their cause.

"... the moment of truth whether the white people really are interested in our welfare or rights."

CHARLES PERKINS
Former FCAATSI Vice-President

In 1962, the Australian Labor Party approached the Liberal-National coalition prime minister, Robert Menzies, for a referendum to ensure First Nations people had representation in the Constitution.

Menzies's refusal made FCAA, now known as FCAATSI, work even harder. Members collected signatures across Australia for petitions asking for changes to Section 51 and the removal of Section 127. In all they gathered enough signatures to create more than 50 petitions. For maximum effect, FCAATSI members presented the petitions to parliament one at a time.

In 1965, First Nations protestors gathered outside Federal Parliament House calling for change to the Constitution. Politicians agreed to meet them. Finally, after years of campaigning, rallying and meetings, the government announced a referendum for 27 May 1967.

The 1967 referendum consisted of three questions. The first asked about changing the numbers in the Senate and the House of Representatives. The second and third were about sections of the Constitution that discriminated against Australia's First Nations people.

In the lead up to the referendum, YES vote supporters held marches, public meetings and rallies and wrote letters to the media asking that all Australians support constitutional change. FCAATSI wanted every Australian, no matter their heritage, to understand why this referendum was important and what a YES vote would mean for Australia's First Nations people.

Finally, after 10 years of campaigning, meetings and collecting signatures, FCAATSI's hard work paid off. On 27 May 1967, more than 90% of Australians voted YES to two of the three referendum questions. The first question about numbers in the Senate and House of Representatives was defeated. However, the questions about changing discrimination against First Nations people were successful. Aboriginal and Torres

EVANS
LANG
LOWE
MACKELLAR
WRONGS
WRITE
YES
ABORIGINES!

Strait Islander people would now be subject to the same laws and regulations as other Australians, and the Australian Government could govern for them.

The 1967 YES vote result is the highest ever received in a Commonwealth referendum.

The successful referendum not only changed how Australia's First Nations people were viewed and governed, it also prompted the government to establish the Office of Aboriginal Affairs and to appoint Australia's first Minister for Aboriginal Affairs, Bill Wentworth. The 1967 referendum also paved the way for the 1975 Racial Discrimination Act. The Act made it illegal to discriminate against a person because of their race.

Opposite: Faith Bandler campaigning at Sydney Town Hall on referendum day, 1967.

WAVE HILL WALK OFF, NORTHERN TERRITORY

23 AUGUST 1966

From its beginning in the late 1800s, the Northern Territory cattle industry relied heavily on Aboriginal workers. Renowned for their skill and knowledge, Aboriginal workers worked as hard, often harder, than white stockman. Aboriginal stockmen were also cheap labour. Instead of paying Aboriginal employees five shillings a day, as the law required, pastoralists paid Aboriginal staff in rations of flour, sugar, meat and accommodation. The rations weren't enough to live on, with the meat usually offcuts, like bullock heads and hoofs. Workers were housed in corrugated-tin huts with dirt floors and no cooking facilities, running water or power.

During the 1930s, a Northern Territory inquiry into the treatment of Aboriginal workers at Wave Hill Cattle Station found its English owner, Lord Vestey, was treating First Nations workers badly. The inquiry recommended Vestey pay workers five shillings a day. Vestey ignored the recommendations and continued paying workers with rations.

In 1965, when the Commonwealth Conciliation and Arbitration Commission agreed landowners must pay equal wages to their Aboriginal staff, First Nations workers were hopeful for change. However, hope turned to anger when the commission deferred payment for three years to ease the financial burden on pastoralists. The commission also introduced a 'slow worker' clause. This allowed landowners to pay a lower wage to any workers they decided weren't working hard enough.

First Nations people were furious. Not only were they still not being paid, but they also feared their bosses would abuse the slow worker rule. Gurindji Elder and Wave Hill head stockman Vincent Lingiari decided to take a stand. On 23 August 1966, Lingiari led 200 stockmen, housemaids and families off the station to the sacred site Daguragu, or Wattie Creek. The Gurindji set up camp and refused to return to work until they received the same conditions and pay as white workers.

Vestey, who believed the Gurindji would return to work when their rations ran out, didn't realise the strikers had support. Dexter Daniels, the Northern Territory Council for Aboriginal Rights President and North Australian Workers' Union Aboriginal organiser, arranged for a Bedford truck filled with supplies to travel from Darwin to Daguragu. During the eight years of the strike, Daniels, Robert Tudawali and Darwin waterfront worker Brian Manning made the 1500-kilometre trip up to 15 times.

"We bin here longa time before them Vestey mob."

VINCENT LINGIARI

As the strike continued and Vestey lost money, he tried to lure strikers back to work. The Gurindji refused his offers. What began as a strike for equal rights and pay soon developed into a fight for the return of traditional land. Rather than work for people who treated them unfairly, the Gurindji people wanted to run their own cattle station on their own Country.

During the strike, Lingiari and other Elders travelled across Australia with Daniels and Communist Party member and writer Frank Hardy. They spoke at public meetings and presented petitions to the Governor-General and Federal Parliament.

After the Labor Party won the 1972 election, the deadlock between the Gurundji people and Vestey broke. Prime Minister Gough Whitlam ordered Vestey to surrender 90 square kilometres of land to the Gurundji people.

Three years later, on 16 August 1975, Prime Minister Whitlam travelled to Daguragu. There he poured soil into Vincent Lingari's hand to symbolise the government's handover of land ownership to the Gurindji people.

The Wave Hill Walk Off lasted eight years. Lingari and the Gurindji people's courage and determination encouraged other First Nations people to stand up for their rights. It also led to the 1976 Commonwealth Lands Act, which recognised Aboriginal land rights.

Opposite: Federal Minister for Aboriginal Affairs, Gordon Bryant, and Wave Hill Walk Off leader Dexter Daniels, Wattie Creek, 1980.

THE TENT EMBASSY, CANBERRA

After the success of the 1967 referendum and the Wave Hill Walk Off, Australia's First Nations people knew they could achieve more. Organisations and activists began to work harder for equal rights for First Nations people, land rights, self-determination and recognition of sovereignty.

The Australian Government didn't share their opinion. On 25 January 1972, Liberal Prime Minister William McMahon announced a new policy rejecting recognition of traditional land ownership, or Aboriginal land rights.

Four First Nations men, Michael Anderson, Billy Craigie, Bertie Williams and Tony Coorey, took immediate action. With a $70 Communist Party grant, the men borrowed a car and drove from the Sydney suburb of Redfern to Parliament House, Canberra. They arrived at one o'clock in the morning on Australia Day and erected a beach umbrella on the lawn opposite Parliament House. The men declared the area an Aboriginal Embassy. They chose the name to symbolise how First Nations people felt like foreigners in their own country.

The protestors announced the embassy was a peaceful and non-violent action to support Aboriginal and Torres Strait Islander people's land rights, preserve sacred sites and for compensation for land taken. The Embassy's slogan was 'One Mob One Voice One Dollar'.

Opposite: Sovereignty sign at the Aboriginal Tent Embassy, Kamberri/Canberra, 2019. Today, the Aboriginal Embassy remains on the lawns outside Old Parliament House

SOVEREIGNTY

By the end of Australia Day, tents of all shapes and sizes surrounded the beach umbrella. First Nations people from across eastern Australia had rushed to join the protest. The area became known as the Tent Embassy. Its prominent position ensured the Tent Embassy attracted attention from local and international media, as well as from tourists visiting Parliament House. The government tried to have the Tent Embassy removed, but a loophole in ACT law allowing up to 12 tents on the lawn made the protest legal.

Protesters tried to meet with the prime minister and other ministers, but all refused. McMahon declared that the protesters didn't represent most Aboriginal people's views. This angered the protestors and increased support for them amongst the Australian community.

On 8 February, Opposition Leader Gough Whitlam met with protest leaders, making him the first politician to visit the Tent Embassy.

Meanwhile, the Government did its best to remove the Tent Embassy. It went as far as to introduce a law that banned camping on unleased Commonwealth land in Canberra. This included the lawn opposite Parliament House.

On 20 July, the day this new law came into effect, police stormed the Tent Embassy, removing tents and people. Days later, despite the violence and arrests, Aboriginal people returned to the lawn and re-established the Tent Embassy. Three days later, police again raided the lawn, and again the protestors returned.

By 30 July, the date of the third police raid, more than 2000 First Nations people were camped at the Tent Embassy. This violent and chaotic raid made national and international headlines. Protest leader Chicka Dixon recalled it as the most violent raid he'd experienced.

"Our land was taken from us by force. Our spiritual beliefs are connected with the land."

MICHAEL ANDERSON

Eventually, the ACT Supreme Court ruled the removal of the Tent Embassy had been illegal. Once again, the Aboriginal Tent Embassy returned to the lawn opposite Parliament House. Many celebrated First Nations activists, including Mum Shirl (Shirley Perry Smith), Gary Foley, Chicka Dixon and Pearl Gibbs, played important roles in the Tent Embassy's success.

Today, the Tent Embassy continues at its original site, although it has been set up at other locations, including Victoria Park, NSW, during the 2000 Sydney Olympics.

Protestors at the Tent Embassy raised the flag that is now recognised as the Aboriginal flag. Designed in 1970 by artist Harold Thomas, the flag, which first flew in Adelaide in 1971, features three colours. The black on the flag represents the people, the red represents the spilt blood and land and the yellow the sun, the source of all life. In 1995, the Australian Government recognised Thomas's design as an official flag.

Since it was first erected on Australia Day 1972, the Tent Embassy has united Australia's First Nations people in the fight for land rights, recognition and equal rights. It has also been the site for memorial services, including one for founder Billy Craigie, and for weddings. Arthur and Rose Kirby married at the Tent Embassy in 1997.

In 1995, the Australian Heritage Commission registered the Tent Embassy on the National Estate.

MABO V QUEENSLAND

Torres Strait Island man Eddie Koiki Mabo was born on Mer (Murray Island) in 1936. Elders exiled 16-year-old Mabo from Mer for breaking island law. On mainland Australia, Mabo worked many jobs, including cutting cane and working on pearl luggers, before becoming a groundsman at James Cook University in Townsville. Here, he earned a reputation as a strong-willed man who stood up for his beliefs and rights.

In 1981, when university lecturers asked Mabo to speak to students about Mer, his world changed. He discovered Mer, which he believed belonged to his people who'd lived there for thousands of years, actually belonged to the Australian Government. A lawyer suggested Mabo take the issue to court. The lawyer lodged a claim against the Queensland Government in May 1982. Though the case was referred to as Mabo V Queensland, four other Mer residents – Celuia Mapo Salee, Sam Passi, Father Dave Passi and James Rice – were part of the challenge.

The long and controversial case questioned the legality of the 1971 terra nullius ruling. Terra nullius is a Latin term that means 'land belonging to no-one'. Europeans used this term when they arrived in Australia to justify the spread of settlement without consulting First Nations people.

The Mabo case argued that as Meriam people had lived in Mer for thousands of years, the island belonged to them. Witness statements and documents supported the argument. The case continued for more than 10 years. Eventually the High Court ruled in Mabo's favour.

Opposite: Eddie Koiki Mabo, Greg McIntyre and Eddie Mabo Jnr, being interviewed on Mer, 1989.

On 3 June 1992, because of Mabo's decision to take the Queensland Government to court, terra nullius was banished from Australian law. This established the foundations of land rights legislation and Native Title in Australia. As well as overruling terra nullius, the High Court acknowledged Australia's First Nations people's ownership of the land and waterways, and their deep spiritual and cultural connection to them.

Five months before the High Court's decision, Eddie Koiki Mabo died from cancer, aged 55. The same year, the Human Rights and Equal Opportunity Commission posthumously awarded Mabo the Australian Human Rights Medal. In 1993, the Australian Government passed the Native Title Act, which not only recognised and protected Native Title, but also outlined the handling of native land claims.

Every year, on 3 June, Torres Strait Island people celebrate Mabo Day with a bank holiday.

Eddie Koiki Mabo wanted to be buried on Mer, however his family chose to bury his body in Townsville. According to custom, three years after Mabo died, his family, friends and media gathered at his grave to erect his tombstone. After they left to celebrate Mabo's life, vandals defaced and graffitied the tombstone. Devastated, the family exhumed Mabo's body and reburied him on Mer.

Opposite: The Commonwealth and Mabo legal teams stop for a feast on Mer, May 1989.

ALWAYS
WAS
ALWAYS
WILL BE

GELAR
META
GED

BRING THE CHILDREN HOME

THE STOLEN GENERATIONS

The first Europeans to arrive in Australia dismissed First Nations people as having nothing to teach them. Many didn't regard First Nations people as human. From 1770, Europeans abused and mistreated Aboriginal people. By the late 1890s, each colony had what were called Aborigines Protection Boards. These boards didn't protect Aboriginal Australians. Rather, the boards removed First Nations people from their traditional lands and forced them to live on missions, stations and reserves. As part of its 'protection' after Federation, the government introduced the assimilation policy.

Assimilation's aim was to make Australia a white nation with one culture and language. Assimilation rules allowed welfare bodies, churches and government organisations to take First Nations children from their families without their parents' consent and, sometimes, their knowledge. Authorities placed the children in institutions or had them fostered by white families. The children were forbidden to contact relatives and banned from their spiritual and cultural practices, including speaking language. Many were told their parents had died or abandoned them. Those with fairer complexions were told they were white.

First Nations children taken to places such as Kinchela Boys Home, Cootamundra, and the Domestic Training Home for Aboriginal Girls were taught to be servants for white people. Girls taken to Cootamundra recalled a sign on the dormitory wall that said, 'Think White, Act White, Be White'.

Opposite: A protest by Grandmothers Against Removals in New South Wales. All over Australia, First Nations people are still protesting for an end to the removal of children from families and communities, which is seen as a continuation of the Stolen Generations.

The forced removal of children from their families and communities continued until 1969, when assimilation policies ended. The policy failed, serving only to create trauma and grief for First Nations children, families and communities. Generations were scarred emotionally and, in many cases, physically. Culture and language were lost.

Government, welfare and church authorities ignored the impact of this forced removal upon the children, their families and communities until the 1980s. At this time, First Nations and non-First Nations people began campaigning for acknowledgement of the removal. During his 1992 speech in Redfern, Sydney, Paul Keating became the first prime minister to acknowledge the forced removal of children, saying, 'We took the children from their mothers.'

Keating's words increased pressure on the government to apologise. In 1997, the Human Rights and Equal Opportunity Commission's Bringing Them Home report highlighted the impact of removing children from their homes. It listed 54 recommendations to help the nation heal and move forward. One of the recommendations was to hold an annual national Sorry Day.

After the Bringing Them Home report, First Nations children taken from their homes and communities became known as the Stolen Generations. According to the report, one in 10 children was taken from their families and communities. Today, many are still searching for their families.

Opposite: Photograph from *Rabbit-Proof Fence* (2002), the film adaptation of Doris (Nugi Garimara) Pilkington's classic book about her mother's removal from her family and her journey home with her sisters.

ALWAYS
WAS
ALWAYS
WILL BE

SORRY DAY

On 26 May 1998, a year after the Human Rights and Equal Opportunity Commission presented the Bringing Them Home report, thousands of Australians from all backgrounds gathered, marched, gave and listened to speeches about the Stolen Generations. This was the first Sorry Day. Participants also signed Sorry Books to acknowledge the mistreatment of Aboriginal and Torres Strait Islander people.

The largest and most spectacular Sorry Day march occurred on 28 May 2000, when more than 250,000 people walked across Sydney Harbour Bridge. This event is known as the Corroboree 2000 Walk for Reconciliation.

In 2005, the National Sorry Day Committee changed the name from Sorry Day to National Day of Healing to highlight the need for healing, as well as an apology.

On 13 February 2008, 10 years after the Bringing Them Home report, Prime Minister Kevin Rudd gave his Apology to Australia's Indigenous People speech. Thousands gathered inside and outside Federal Parliament to hear the historic apology. Rudd's speech acknowledged the wrongs committed against First Nations people since European colonisation. Most importantly, he apologised to the Stolen Generations.

> **"For the pain, suffering and hurt of these Stolen Generations, their descendants and for their families left behind, we say sorry."**
>
> **KEVIN RUDD**
> **13 February 2008**

The government also announced plans to improve Australia's First Nations people's living conditions. It adapted Oxfam's Close the Gap campaign to suit Australia and to help reduce the gap in education, health and living standards between Australia's First Nations people and non-First Nations people.

Today the gap still exists. As a nation we still have a long way to go to heal and rebuild relationships, but the acknowledgement of the Stolen Generations and the apology were a start.

Opposite: The 'Sea of Hands' is a popular way that community members show support and solidarity for First Nations people during national events.

Be
Brave.
Make
Change.

Speed kills.
Speed kills.
Speed kills.

THE LONG WALK

Michael Long is best known for his success playing Australian Rules Football (AFL). Between 1989 and 2001, Long played 190 games for Essendon. He played in two premierships and, in 1993, won the Norm Smith Medal for the player judged to be best on ground during the AFL grand final.

As well as being a successful and respected AFL player, Long fought racism within the league. After a racist incident during the 1995 Anzac Day game between Collingwood and Essendon, the quietly spoken Long challenged the AFL to introduce a racial abuse code. This was to be the first code of its kind in AFL history. Today, it is regarded as the beginning of Long's public dedication to First Nations affairs.

After retiring, Long was devastated by the number of funerals for friends and loved ones he'd had to attend in a short space of time. He decided to use his profile to draw attention to the issues facing First Nations communities. He vowed to meet with Prime Minister John Howard, even if he had to walk to Canberra to do so.

True to his word, on 21 November 2004, Long left his Melbourne home bound for Parliament House, Canberra. His aim was to not only meet with Howard, but to raise awareness about conditions in Aboriginal and Torres Strait Islander communities. Thousands of First Nations and non-First Nations Australians joined Long on his walk. Some walked the entire journey with him, others walked a short way. All helped him achieve his goal. This support and encouragement turned Long's walk into a message of hope. After 11 days and 650 kilometres, Long arrived in Canberra on 2 December. He met with Prime Minister Howard the following day.

Opposite: Michael Long being chaired off the ground after the round 13 match between Essendon and Western Bulldogs, Naarm/Melbourne, 1999.

LONG WALK
THE LONG WALK

Long's trek inspired The Long Walk charity, which raises awareness of issues affecting Aboriginal and Torres Strait Islander people. It also supports education programs, such as Walk the Talk, and cultural exchanges designed to inform and heal.

The Long Walk has taken place every year since Long's first trek. In 2023, Long once again walked from Melbourne, Wurundjeri Country, to Canberra, Ngunnawal-Ngambri Country. This time he completed the walk to support a YES vote in the 2023 Voice to Parliament referendum. Long is recognised not only for his football skills and leadership, but also as a dedicated and hardworking advocate for First Nations people's rights and affairs.

The Long Walk participants cross the Matagarup Bridge, Boorloo/Perth, 2021.

RECONCILIATION

The fight for equal treatment and rights for Australia's First Nations people has come a long way since Federation. But it still has a long way to go. Today, the fight has become more corporate, with many groups advocating for change and with a committment to raising awareness.

Reconciliation Australia is an independent non-government organisation that aims to build relationships, respect and trust between the wider Australian community and Aboriginal and Torres Strait Islander people.

Reconciliation Australia was established in 2001, 10 years after its predecessor, the Council for Reconciliation, began its work. Australia runs programs in schools, workplaces, universities and community groups to challenge and change the discrimination that still exists in Australia. National Reconciliation Week is an annual campaign to highlight this work.

Reconciliation Australia believes the process of reconciliation is made up of five areas: race relations, unity, institutional integrity, historical acceptance and equality and equity. Reconciliation, according to Reconciliation Australia, is not a single issue or agenda. Rather, reconciliation must weave all of these threads together.

Many people remember the massive bridge walks in 2000. An estimated 250,000 people took part in the Sydney Harbour Bridge walk and other demonstrations around the country. These events were the beginning of the transition from the Council to Reconciliation. Reconciliation Australia also led the Recognise campaign. This campaign, launched in 2012 by Prime Minister Julia Gillard, sought to educate people about parts of the Constitution that discriminate against First Nations people. It aimed to raise awareness of the need for Constitutional change, just as those who fought for a YES vote in the 1967 Referendum did. Currently the Constitution doesn't mention Australia's First Nations people or their connection to the land, which has continued for more than 65,000 years.

The Recognise campaign ended in 2017. That same year, 250 people attended the First Nations National Constitutional Convention at Uluru. The Convention followed months of discussions with communities across Australia about constitutional recognition.

After the National Constitutional Convention, the delegates released the Uluru Statement from the Heart. The statement highlights hopes for real change that will recognise and make a difference for Australia's First Nations People. Reconciliation Australia supports the Uluru Statement from the Heart and continues to campaign for change to the Australian Constitution.

For reconciliation to be effective, Reconciliation Australia believes Australia must actively address inequality and injustice. It must also act where the rights of First Nation people are ignored, denied or diminished. To do this, as a country, Australia needs to address racism in all of its forms.

ALWAYS WAS
ALWAYS WILL BE
ABORIGINAL
LAND
ABOLISH
AUSTRALIA
NEVER
CEDED
STOP KILLING US
I DONT WANT TO BE
ANOTHER STATISTIC
AUSTRALIA DOES
NOT EXIST
STILL HERE
STILL HERE
STILL HERE
STILL HERE

WORDS, ART AND MUSIC

Australia's First Nations people have an oral tradition. Unlike Western cultures that rely on the written word, Aboriginal and Torres Strait Islander people have always shared and recorded their history, laws, culture and traditions through songs, stories, art and dance. It's not surprising that Australia's First Nations people use these forms to protest and call for change.

First Nations people have written award-winning poetry and novels about their lives and experiences. Poets such as Oodgeroo Noonuccal and Kevin Gilbert wrote about civil rights, Country and racism. They also took part in demonstrations and protests such as the Tent Embassy. In recent times, reporter, journalist and Wiradjuri man Stan Grant has written books about racism in Australia and how, as a nation, Australia needs to change.

Aboriginal and Torres Strait Islander singer/songwriters write about their own experiences and observations. In telling their stories, they show the Australian community the effect of the Stolen Generations, the meaning of Country and how First Nations people have been and continue to be treated. Archie Roach's song, Took the Children Away, opened non-First Nations people's eyes to the damage done by Stolen Generations. One of Kev Carmody's many songs, From Little Things Big Things Grow, co-written with Paul Kelly, is the story of Vincent Lingiari and the Wave Hill Walk Off. Opera singer Deborah Cheetham writes songs in traditional languages and has written and performed operas about early colonisation, including Eumerella, A War Requiem for Peace.

Opposite: Poster by Wiradjuri and Ngiyampaa artist Charlotte Allingham made for an Australia Day protest, 2020.

First Nations bands have written songs about what they call the 'blackfella experience'. The No Fixed Address song, We Have Survived, is a celebration of the resilience and courage of First Nations people. The Warumpi Band's Blackfella/Whitefella is an anti-racism anthem. These bands and others, including Coloured Stone, wrote music that people loved and told stories that made people stop and think.

In the early 1990s, Yothu Yindi became a national and international success. The band, singing in Yolngu-Matha language and English, played traditional instruments, including yidakis and clapsticks. They sang about the need for a treaty and a united voice. As well as changing people's opinions, they introduced many to Yolngu culture.

Today's First Nation singer/songwriters, including Briggs, A.B. Original, Dan Sultan, Baker Boy and Jessie Lloyd from the Mission Songs Project, continue to write music that challenges, inspires and shares First Nations experiences.

In the visual arts field, First Nations artists, including painters and photographers, have shown audiences how mistreatment has affected clans and nations. At the same time, these artists have been able to share their culture with a wide audience. William Barak's paintings of traditional Wurundjeri life and ceremony have helped preserve the traditions, while also showing what has been lost.

The Ngurrara Canvas is a powerful example of art as protest. Ngurrara Elders created the enormous painting to show their connection to Country. The painting helped them win a Native Title claim in 1997.

These are only a handful of examples of how First Nations people have used art, music and stories to create change. First Nations people also used letters, petitions, rallies and strikes to send a strong message to those in power. But First Nations people's storytelling through art, dance and song, show how behaviours have impacted on communities and what needs to change. Creative activism, as it's sometimes called, allows everyone, not just those in power, to listen to or see a situation differently.

> **"When you've got art, you've got voice, when you've got voice you've got freedom and with freedom comes responsibility."**
>
> **RICHARD FRANKLAND**

Y
E
S

VOICE REFERENDUM

After the 2017 First Nations Constitutional Convention, the supporters of the Uluru Statement from the Heart requested that a First Nations Voice be enshrined in the Australian Constitution. This Voice, or the Voice to Parliament as it became known, would be an advisory group made up of Aboriginal and Torres Strait Islander people. First Nations people would elect representatives from their communities to be part of this group, and those elected members would review all new laws affecting Aboriginal and Torres Strait Islander people.

The group would offer feedback to the government. Basically, the Voice to Parliament would give Aboriginal and Torres Strait Islander people a say in their own lives. Enshrining the Voice to Parliament in the Constitution would mean the advisory body couldn't be removed by future governments.

In 2022, newly elected Labor Prime Minister Anthony Albanese announced a referendum to decide if the Voice to Parliament would be added to the Australian Constitution. Constitutional change requires the Australian Government to hold a referendum, as it did in 1967. For the referendum to be successful, the results must be a double majority, which means a YES vote of more than 50% of voters along with a majority YES vote in four of the six Australian states.

In the lead up to the 14 October referendum, First Nations leaders campaigned tirelessly to explain what the Voice to Parliament would mean and why it was needed. This YES campaign, made up of 300 community groups and 60,000 volunteers, based its message in positivity and good will.

Opposite: Protesters holding up signs in Victoria Gardens at the end of the YES walk, Boorloo/Perth, 2023.

Media about the campaign tended to spread fear, negativity and misinformation about the Voice. During the campaign, incidents of racism and prejudice against First Nations people increased. Unfortunately, the YES campaign was unsuccessful, with most of Australia voting NO to a change to the Constitution.

Despite the result, organisers were encouraged by the 6.2 million people who voted Yes. After the result, a group of anonymous First Nations leaders released a statement which said, 'This is a bitter irony. That people who have only been on this continent for 235 years would refuse to recognise those whose home this land has been for 60,000 and more years is beyond reason.'

Beaten but unbowed, Aboriginal and Torres Strait Islander leaders declared they would continue to fight for a better future for their people.

Opposite: Supporters with signs begin the YES walk over the Matagarup Bridge, Boorloo/ Perth, 2023.

VOTE
YES!
yes23
RESPECT to
the ELDERS
who ASKED
to be HEARD
YES

CONCLUSION

From the time Europeans first arrived at Botany Bay, Aboriginal and Torres Strait Islanders have been mistreated, abused and stripped of their land. While the newcomers sought to establish a democracy that gave citizens the freedom to worship, vote, and speak as they wish, the civil rights they established for themselves were denied to First Nations people.

Bit by bit, courageous and dedicated Aboriginal and Torres Strait Islander people have clawed back what was taken and what was denied. Through courage and determination, Australia's First Nations People achieved basic rights, including the right to be recognised as citizens of the nation, the right to vote and the right to equal pay. Each protest has been a stepping stone to the next battle.

Even though advances have been made, much is yet to be achieved. Understanding the past helps us see how far we have come. It also shows us how we to continue to work towards healing and understanding between First Nations and non-First Nations Australians.

GLOSSARY

Activist: A person who works hard to achieve change for a political or social situation.

Apartheid: A political system that existed in South Africa and South West Africa (now Namibia) that separated white people from people of colour.

Assimilation: To make people stop their own cultural practices and become part of another community or culture.

Census: A count or survey of a population, conducted to collect information.

Chief Secretary: Name for the head of the Victorian Government from 1855–1936. After 1936, the title Chief Secretary changed to Premier.

Civil Rights: The rights of all people to be treated equally, no matter their skin colour, sex, religion or political views.

Constitution: The fundamental principles outlining how a country is to be governed and the rights and obligations of a country's citizens.

Double Majority: A YES vote in a referendum of more than 50% and a majority YES vote in four of six Australian states.

Federation: The uniting of separate colonies into a nation.

Land Rights: The rights of Aboriginal and Torres Strait Islander people to land.

Native Title: Recognises Aboriginal people and Torres Strait Islanders have rights and interests in the land and that the land is directly linked to their laws and customs.

Non-government organisation (NGO): An organisation that operates independently from the government, usually as a non-profit organisation. Often an NGO operates with a humanitarian or social change mission.

Ngurungaeta: The Wurundjeri language, Woi-Wurrung, word for the leader or head of a clan.

Referendum: A compulsory vote that asks the public for its opinion on a particular change to the Constitution.

Pastoralists: Landowners raising sheep or cattle.

Stolen Generations: Name given to First Nations children removed from their families and communities between 1890 and 1970.

Terra nullius: Latin term meaning 'land belonging to no-one'.

PICTURE CREDITS

Cover, page 1 and featured throughout Clothing The Gaps. We thank Clothing The Gaps for granting permission to use their sticker collection artwork.

Pages 4–5 & 10 Maree Clarke, M00000050 Photograph #28 and M00000019 Photograph #17, from the *Living Archive of Aboriginal Art online exhibition.* Image provided courtesy of the artist.

Page 8 Natalie Ironfield, 'Stop Killing Our People, Stop Taking Our Future' 2019 Invasion Day Rally, Victorian Parliament Steps, Wurundjeri Country.

Page 13 Algernon Talmage (1937) 'The Founding of Australia by Capt. Arthur Phillip R.N. Sydney Cove, Jan. 26th 1788'.

Page 15 'Aboriginal Australians, Coranderrk'. State Library of Victoria.

Page 16 Carl Walker (1866). William Barak -- age 33. State Library of Victoria.

Page 19 Carl Walter (1860). Frontview of the Coranderrk Aboriginal Village. State Library of Victoria.

Page 20 and **23** Jimmy Clements' protest at Parliament House (1927) provided by Trove, National Library of Australia.

Page 24 Aborigines Day of Mourning (1938). Published Mar–Apr. 1938, in Man Magazine, Sydney, NSW. Mitchell Collection, State Library of NSW.

Page 27 Courtesy of the descendants of William Cooper.

Page 33 Courtesy of the descendants of William Cooper.

Page 36 Tobias Titz in collaboration with Wangka Maya Pilbara Aboriginal Language Centre. 'Teddy Allan and Dylan Corbett comment on the Pilbara Strike, 2009'. Writing by the subjects.

Page 41 FCAATSI Right Wrongs Write Yes for Aborigines poster. State Library of New South Wales.

Page 42 Pearl Gibbs and Faith Bandler images provided by the State Library of New South Wales.

Page 45 George Lipman (1967). Harriet Ellis 27 May 1967. *Sydney Morning Herald.*

Page 46 Charles Perkins image provided by State Library of NSW.

Page 52 George Lipman (1967). Faith Bandler at the Sydney Town Hall 27 May 1967. *Sydney Morning Herald.*

Page 56 National Archives of Australia.

Page 59 Rafael Ben-Ari (2019). Aboriginal Tent Embassy.

Page 62 & 65 Courtesy of Trevor Graham and Yarra Bank Films.

Page 66 Courtesy **of** Richard Milnes licensed through Alamy Stock Photos.
69 Courtesy of Phillip Noyce (2002). Page 69 is a Still from *Rabbit-Proof Fence* used with permission.

Page 70 Photograph by Natalie Ironfield, 'Stop Killing Our People, Stop Taking Our Future' 2019 Invasion Day Rally, Victorian Parliament Steps, Wurundjeri Country.

Page 70–71 Maree Clarke, "M00000019 Photograph #28," from the *Living Archive of Aboriginal Art online exhibition*. Image provided courtesy of the artist.

Page 73 Courtesy of Reconciliation Australia.

Page 74 Stuart Milligan/ALLSPORT (1999). Licensed by Getty Images.

Page 76–77 Brynn O'Connor (2021). Courtesy of Reconciliation Australia.

Page 80 Charlotte Allingham/Coffinbirth (2019). Image courtesy of the artist.

Pages 84 & 87 Courtesy of Cole Baxter.

Back cover: Dexter Daniels and Captain Major at Australia Square job site meeting, 14 October 1966. Mitchell Library, State Library of NSW and courtesy of SEARCH Foundation.

REFERENCES

The authors acknowledge the information and resources listed.

A warning that some of these websites include actual footage of events as well as images of Aboriginal and Torres Strait Islander people who have passed away.

AIATSIS public website and resources list. **http://aiatsis.gov.au.**

ABC Radio National. The Art Show. "Aboriginal Resistance, Healing and Matriarchy." 20 Nov. 2019.

AIATSIS. *The Little Red Yellow Black Book: An Introduction to Indigenous Australia*. Aboriginal Studies Press, 2018.

Atkinson, Uncle Wayne. Not One Iota: The Yorta Yorta Struggle for Land Justice. PhD Thesis, La Trobe University, 2000.

Blackshaw, Adam. "Student Action for Aborigines Protests." National Film and Sound Archive of Australia. 2023, **https://www.nfsa.gov.au/latest/dr-perkins-and-1965-freedom-ride.**

Broome, Richard. *Australian Aboriginals: A History Since 1788*. 4th ed., Allen and Unwin, 2010.

Butler, Dan. "Explainer: Day of Mourning, the birth of modern First Nations protest." NITV, 20 Jan. 2020.

Goodall, Heather. *Invasion to Embassy: Land in Aboriginal Politics in NSW, 1770-1972*. Allen & Unwin in association with Black Books, 1996.

Murray, Ngarra. "My grandfather protested against Australia Day in 1938. We'll never have a reason to rejoice on that day." ABC News, 24 Jan. 2018.

Noakes, David, director. *How the West Was Lost: The Story of the 1946 Aboriginal Pastoral Workers' Strike*. 1987.

Norris, Nathan. "Forgotten Legacy of Aboriginal Stockwomen Becomes Subject of PhD Research." ABC Goldfields, 2018.

Pascoe, Bruce. *Convincing Ground: Learning to Fall in Love with Your Country*. Aboriginal Studies Press, 2012.

Pascoe, Bruce. *Dark Emu*. Magabala Books, 2019.

Perkins, Rachel, and Beck Cole, directors. *The First Australians*. Blackfella Films, 2008.

Patten, J. T., and W. Ferguson. "Aborigines Claim Citizen Rights." Aborigines Progressive Association, 1938.

Ross, Monique. "Indigenous Music: Kev Carmody, Archie Roach and Peter Garrett talk Aboriginal Protest Songs." ABC News, 3 Nov. 2016, **https://www.abc.net.au/news/2016-11-03/indigenous-protest-songs-kev-carmody-archie-roach-peter-garrett/7949334.**

Scrimgeour, Ann. *On red earth walking: the Pilbara Aboriginal Strike*, Western Australia 1946–1949. Monash University Publishing, 2020.

Torres, Mitchell. *Jandamarra's War*. Screenwest, 2011.

Woorunmurra, Banjo, and Howard Pedersen. *Jandamarra and the Bunuba Resistance*. Magabala Books, 1995.

"Aborigines Meet, Mourn, While White Man Celebrates." *Man Magazine*, Mar. 1938.

"Our Historic Day of Mourning and Protest." *The Abo Call*, Apr. 1938.

"Our Ten Points." *The Abo Call*, Apr. 1938.

The Maloga petition, 1881.

"The People In That Picture." *Koori Mail*, 14 Jul. 2004.

"Students lead 'Freedom Ride' through NSW towns." Deadly Story, **https://deadlystory.com/page/culture/history/Students_lead_%E2%80%98Freedom_Rides%E2%80%99_through_segregated_NSW_towns.**

ABOUT THE AUTHORS

Aunty Fay Muir
Aunty Fay Stewart Muir is a senior Boon Wurrung and Wamba Wamba Elder, First Nations community leader and Koori Court Elder. She is a Language Specialist, working as a prison educator in First Nations languages and is a creative language revival consultant and collaborator.

Aunty Fay provides cultural guidance to students and teachers at all levels of the Victorian education system, providing cultural and curriculum advice. In 2020, she was inducted to both the Victorian Honour Roll of Women and the Victorian Aboriginal Honour Roll. Aunty Fay cares about sharing her culture and stories and loves to take readers on a journey of learning.

Sue Lawson
Award-winning Australian author Sue Lawson writes books for children and young adults. Her books include *The Biscuit Maker*, illustrated by Liz Anelli and young adult novels *Freedom Ride*, shortlisted for the Children's Book Council of Australia Book of the Year and the NSW and WA Premier's Literary Awards, and *Pan's Whisper*, which won the Australian Family Therapist Award and was shortlisted for the Prime Minister's Literary Award.

Sue's young adult and children's books are recognised for the sensitive way they explore the exciting and heartbreaking complexities of growing up.

Fay and Sue's first book together was *Nganga: Aboriginal and Torres Strait Islander Words and Phrases*.

Since then, they have collaborated on three books, *Respect*, *Family* and *Sharing*, co-written as part of the Magabala 'Our Place' series.

MORE FROM MAGABALA BOOKS

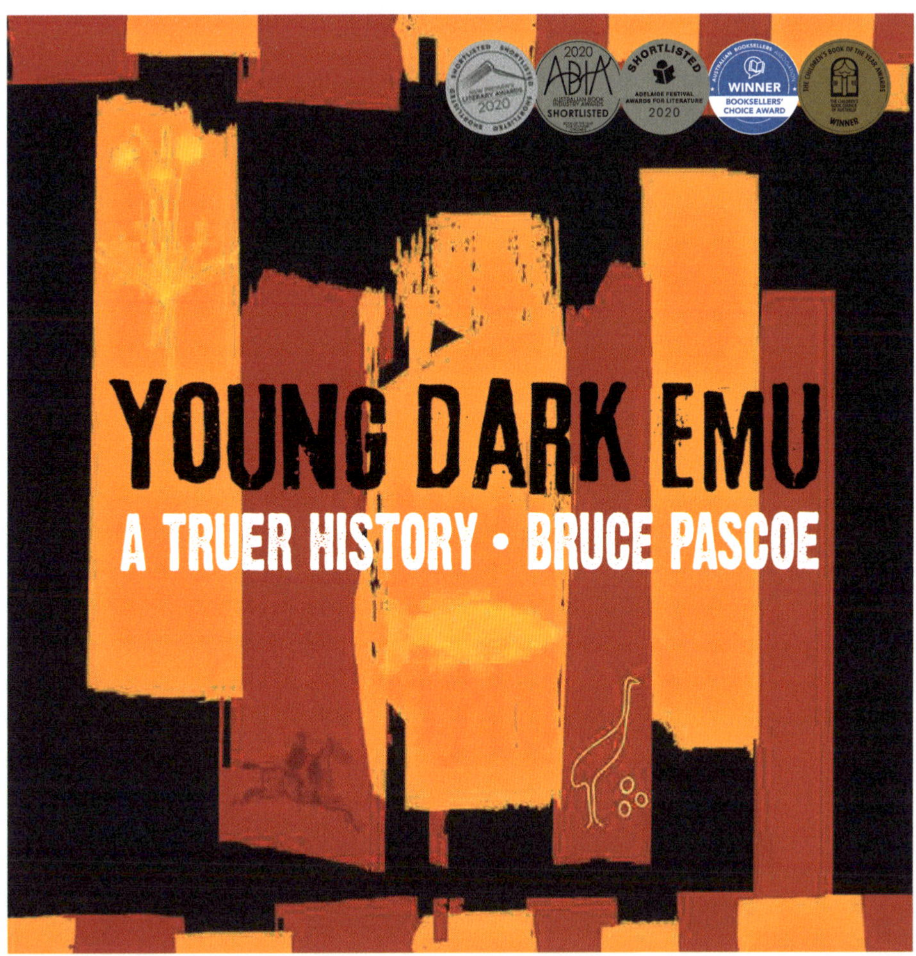

Praise for Young Dark Emu

"...this book should be required reading for all - it is a gift of knowledge we should all be grateful for."
– *Australian Geographic Explorers*

"Stunningly presented in striking shades of ochre, orange, black and white, this seminal book invites young readers to contemplate a different picture of Aboriginal culture and the concept of terra nullius."
– *Dr Stephanie Owen Reeder, The Canberra Times*

ALWAYS WAS ALWAYS WILL BE

PAY THE RENT

TREATY NOW

TELL THE TRUTH

TREATY NOW

CHANGE THE DATE WE STILL WONT CELEBRATE

this Land has a black future

ABORIGINES CLAIM CITIZEN RIGHTS!

ABORIGINES CONFERENCE

DAY of MOURNING

HANDS OFF BLAK KIDS

PAY THE RENT

TELL THE TRUTH

TREATY NOW

ALWAYS WAS ALWAYS WILL BE